Kill Clock

by

Allan Guthrie

First published in 2007 in Great Britain by
Barrington Stoke Ltd
18 Walker St, Edinburgh, EH3 7LP

www.barringtonstoke.co.uk

ISBN: 978-1-84299-499-3

Printed in Great Britain by Bell & Bain Ltd

Barrington Stoke acknowledges subsidy from the Scottish
Arts Council towards the publication of this volume

Scottish
Arts Council

A Note from the Author

My first novel, *Two-Way Split*, was about an Edinburgh hard man called Pearce. A nice enough guy, as long as you don't get on his bad side. He's tough but fair. He only kills people who deserve it!

I carried on with his story in another novel, *Hard Man*. There were some characters from the first book, though, who still interested me, and I wanted to explore them a little further. *Kill Clock* was a great chance to do just that.

So here we find Pearce taking his three-legged dog for a walk on the beach. Before long, his peace will be shattered by the police, ex-girlfriends, death threats, loan sharks, kidnappings, guns, two small children, and a midnight meeting that's a matter of life and death.

I hope you enjoy reading *Kill Clock* as much as I enjoyed writing it.

For my mum

Contents

Tick Tock ...
7:30 pm

An April evening in Portobello, Edinburgh's seaside. A light rain keeping it damp, a nippy breeze keeping it cool.

Scotland's weather was good on the whole. Apart from the summer when Gordon Pearce got too hot. Nothing worse than the sun on your skin, making your armpits prickle and your back as wet as a river-bed.

But, no, it was spring, and here he was, walking down to the beach in his T-shirt.

Taking his three-legged dog, Hilda, for a walk.

The closer they got to the beach, the cooler it became. Sea breezes could sometimes sting. But this was refreshing. As good as a cold shower.

At the bottom of the road, just as Pearce and his dog were crossing over to the beach, a black car backed out of its parking space right in front of them. The car stopped with a jolt, the rear bumper about a foot away from Pearce's legs.

Pearce didn't own a car, and this kind of behaviour pissed him off.

He didn't know much about cars. Didn't know the make of this one. Just knew that the driver had nearly run them over and was tooting his horn at them.

Prick.

Well, maybe the guy was trying to signal a mate who was still in the pub across the street. Maybe that's what the horn-tooting was all about. Pearce looked in that direction but no-one came out.

Pearce could have moved, walked round the side of the car. But he didn't see why he should. He was on the road first.

The horn blared again. The driver lowered his window, stuck his head out. It was an odd shape, like a peanut, and just as bald. He looked behind him.

"Fucking move," the guy said to Pearce, blasting the horn three times.

Pearce didn't budge. Hilda tugged the lead and whined. Pearce spoke to him out the side of his mouth "It's OK. This won't take me long."

Oh, yeah. Hilda was a 'he'. Named after Pearce's mother, who'd died violently a few years ago. That's not to say Pearce thought his mother was a bitch. Far from it. They'd been close. Which was why he'd named the dog after her.

Now, it wasn't as if Pearce had suddenly stopped in the middle of the road. He'd been crossing at an even pace. And when he'd set foot off the pavement, there was no traffic. This peanut-headed arse-hole had pulled out without looking. Or maybe it was on purpose. Which was even worse.

The driver stuck his head out of the car window again, and said, "Why the fuck don't you move? And take your stupid dog with you."

What the fuck was wrong with him? Why couldn't he just be polite? These days, everyone was a rude fuck.

Pearce didn't move.

The guy shook his head. Leaned on the horn.

Two punters came out of the pub to see what was going on.

The driver let his hand off the horn and said to Pearce, "You've got ten seconds to get out of the way." He started counting. "Ten … nine … eight …"

Pearce bent down, picked up Hilda, stood his ground, stared at the guy in the car.

"… three … two … one," the guy in the car said.

What was he going to do now?

The car backed up slowly.

Pearce watched it come closer, wondering how far this slap-head was prepared to go. He found out when the bumper touched his shins. Pearce pressed against the car, but knew he wasn't going to be a match for it. He took two steps back and moved off to the side.

He placed Hilda on the ground, a safe distance from the reversing car. The beach was only yards away. The grassy area where Hilda did his business was nearby. Pearce un-clipped the lead, said to the dog, "Go, be busy."

The car crept backwards. As it came along-side Pearce, the driver shouted through the open window: "I've a good mind to take your fucking dog and shove it up your arse."

Pearce leaned towards him. The guy stared at Pearce a second, then rolled up the window.

Pearce could have reached in and grabbed the fucker. But he let him raise the window. More fun that way.

With the window up, the guy was feeling brave again. Started calling Pearce names, thinking he was safe with the pane of glass between them. But none-the-less he was giving it laldy. Flecks of spit collected in the corners of his mouth.

He should have driven away.

Pearce leaned back, turned to the side and kicked his heel into the glass. A fine mess it made.

Inside the car tiny bits of glass fell in a shower over the driver. He yelled and Pearce could hear him clearly now, surprised, scared that he was hurt.

The window was gone.

Pearce looked over at Hilda, who was squatting, back towards him as always. Until he'd got Hilda, Pearce hadn't known that a dog could be shit-shy.

But Pearce wasn't finished with the prick in the car.

Pearce put his hands on the bonnet, jumped up onto it. Had to bend over to see the guy inside. He'd been brushing bits of glass off himself and had cut himself. He was sucking his finger, but he stopped and looked up when Pearce thumped down in front of him.

7

Yep. There was a madman standing on his car. At least, Pearce guessed that's how it seemed to him. The driver wasn't being so mouthy, anyway.

Pearce didn't stop to think. He drove his foot into the wind-screen. And felt it in his heel. Pretty solid fucker. The blow only resulted in a crack.

Inside, the driver cowered.

Pearce kicked the wind-screen again. Bigger crack, and something gave.

Third time, the wind-screen spider-webbed. Good enough. No way the fucker would be able to see out of that.

Pearce jumped down. Content to leave it at that.

But this bald bastard was a real twat.

The slap-head opened the door, glass falling onto the road. "You cunt," he said. "Look what you've fucking done."

By now, the two guys who'd come out of the pub had been joined by a bunch more people to watch the fun and games. They'd only expected a game of pool tonight, so this was a real bonus.

The slap-head shook his arms. Bits of glass dropped to the ground. He looked at Pearce. "I'm gonna ..."

"What?" Pearce said.

No reply. What a surprise.

Pearce walked away.

He hadn't gone far when he heard the car engine. He turned as the car reversed towards him. Stopped short. Again.

The slap-head braked, shouted, "You're fucking paying for this."

Pearce walked round the side of the car, opened the door, reached inside. The prick put his arms up to protect himself. Pearce grabbed him. Pulled him out, sent him

9

sprawling onto the road. Pearce looked at the spray of glass on the driver's seat. There was a coat in the passenger seat. He reached in, picked it up, placed it on the driver's seat. Then climbed inside and sat on the coat.

"Hey," the driver said, jumping to his feet. "What are you doing?"

Pearce closed the door.

The driver shoved his hand through the hole where the window used to be.

Pearce grabbed his hand and used the guy's momentum to pull him forward. His face bounced off the roof of the car.

That hurt.

Pearce let go.

The engine was still running. Pearce had to remind himself about the business of driving all over again. Been a long time since he'd been behind a wheel. Hadn't had much experience before he went to jail, and obviously he didn't do much driving there. Since he'd come out, he hadn't had the need.

First thing, he put on his seat-belt.

Then he pressed in the clutch, found first gear and applied a little power. The soles of his boots were pretty thick. Not the best for driving with. But that didn't really matter. There was only one thing on his mind.

About twenty feet to the left was the wall of the local bus station.

Pearce stepped on the accelerator and headed towards it. Hard to see through the cracked wind-screen, but he was aware of the general direction.

He had fun rushing forward for a few seconds, and then ...

BANG.

About twenty miles an hour when he hit. Caught the wall a little side-on.

The impact jarred, but he'd felt worse.

He turned off the engine, took out the keys. Un-clipped his belt. Stepped out to inspect the damage.

Nice.

The whole of the front driver's side was caved in. Steam was coming out of the bonnet. Water from the burst radiator dripping onto the road. The bumper was bent in a V-shape.

The car's owner hadn't moved.

Pearce stepped towards him, lobbed him the keys.

The prick didn't even bother trying to catch them, just looked at the ground where they'd fallen.

7:45 pm

Someone must have phoned the police. Pearce could hear sirens.

He called Hilda, put the lead back on him, started for home. Brushed past a couple of drunk idiots on the pavement in front of the pub. The taller one, who stank of beer and sweat, said, "Nice car you just pranged."

Pearce slowed down enough to grunt.

The drunk guy said, "Jamie ain't happy."

Jamie must be the slap-head who owned the car. Pearce said, "Fuck Jamie."

The other drunk guy, who had a ginger moustache, said, "Don't think Jamie's wife would like that." And the pair of drunks started to laugh.

Pearce pulled Hilda away from sniffing the ginger guy's shoe and headed back home up the road. A police car turned off the roundabout, drove slowly down the street, past Pearce, towards the scene of the accident.

The last thing Pearce wanted was to get mixed up with the police. He really didn't get on with them.

8:00 pm

"Pearce?"

Someone had called his name. The voice sounded familiar. But Pearce couldn't think who it belonged to. He turned just as a woman opened her car door, hung out of it, one strappy wine-red-sandalled foot on the ground. She was maybe in her early 30s. Tiny, slim, delicate, pale, dyed blonde hair. She wasn't bad looking if you were into the crack whore look.

Didn't do much for Pearce, though. He hated drugs. Ever since his sister died of an over-dose.

"Yep," he said, looking into her eyes, trying to work out what she wanted.

"You don't recognise me?" she said. She raised her cigarette to her lips. A real anger about the way she puffed on it. Eyes screwed up, lips clamped round the butt, skin pulled tight across her cheek-bones.

She shook her head slightly. Pearce remembered the movement. Only he'd known her when her hair was jet black.

"Julie?" he said.

She grinned. Smoke curled out through her teeth. She hadn't smoked when they were engaged.

"What do you want?" Pearce asked, stepping towards her. He forced back a rising anger. "Haven't seen you in ..."

"Over six years," she finished for him. She shifted about a bit, pointed her toes, took another drag. She said, "Get in."

"Don't think so," he said.

"Come on," she said. "I need your help."

Pearce wouldn't normally have hopped into a car with an ex-girlfriend. Not one who'd ripped him off like Julie had. But it was as good a way as any of hiding from the police. And she couldn't rip him off again, since this time he already knew what she was like.

As he got closer, Pearce saw that she wasn't alone in the car. There were two kids in the back. Julie had been busy since he'd last seen her. He couldn't tell their ages. Might as well have asked him the age of a random pair of sheep. Looked like a boy and a girl, although even that wasn't clear. What was clear was that they both looked tired and stroppy.

Pearce walked round to the other side. Hilda perked up his ears, no doubt wondering why they weren't going home as usual. Julie leaned across, pushed the door open. Pearce hesitated. Then bent down, picked up Hilda.

He brushed some sweetie wrappers off the seat, sat down. "What do you want with me?" he asked Julie.

As soon as Pearce spoke, the kid who looked like a boy started to cry.

Julie said, "Shut it, Kirk."

Then the other kid kicked off.

"They yours?" Pearce asked.

"Aye," Julie said. "Worse luck." She switched her fag into her other hand, reached into the back and gave Kirk a crack across the legs.

That slap made Kirk cry all the louder. Which made his sister cry louder too. Pearce was fairly sure she was a girl now. There were dolls and a fairy wand on her side of the back seat.

Julie said to her children, "You pair of cunts shut the fuck up or you'll get put outside. What the fuck's the noise all about anyway?"

After a second, Kirk said, "The man."

"The man," his sister said.

"What man? This man?" Julie looked at Pearce. "He's a friend of mine. He's going to help." She kept looking at Pearce.

After a second, Pearce saw that she was waiting for him to back her up.

"Aye," he said. "I'm a pal. No need to cry. I'm not going to hurt you or touch you up or anything."

Julie looked at him strangely.

"What?" he said. He was proud of himself, getting them to shut up without threatening to hit them. Unlike their mother. Didn't know what she was looking at him like that for. He could give her some lessons in parenting. It wasn't that hard, really.

She took another drag of her fag, tossed it out the window, let loose a stream of smoke that seemed never-ending. At last, she said, "Don't joke about touching them up."

"I wasn't joking. I said I wasn't going to. I was serious."

"You don't say things like that in front of kids."

"No? Well, how would I know?"

She asked, "You don't have any kids?"

"No," Pearce said. "Haven't exactly had the chance."

"Look," she said. "About what happened ..."

"Forget it," he said. "I have."

"OK," she said.

* * *

Six years ago. Pearce hadn't been out of prison long and they'd only known each other two weeks. He should have known better. But he didn't. He'd thought she cared for him. She'd strung him along so fucking easily it was embarrassing. He'd borrowed a stack of money from a loan shark to buy a very expensive diamond ring for their engagement. Once she'd got it on her finger, Julie had vanished. Without a trace. He'd spoken to her only once after that. On the phone. Well, it wasn't really speaking. They'd shouted at one another.

"I should go," Pearce said. "Before I say something else out of place." He put his hand on the door handle.

"Doggie's got a leg missing." That was the little girl speaking.

21

Pearce turned, looked over his shoulder into the back.

The girl was drooling all over a headless doll in her lap. She pointed at Hilda and said, "How does it walk?"

Pearce said, "Easy. Just puts one paw in front of the other."

"That's funny!" she giggled.

Kirk said, "Doesn't he fall over?"

"Hardly ever," Pearce said.

"Can he run?"

"Like Linford Christie."

"Who?"

Pearce looked at Julie. "Yeah," she said. "Who?"

"Doesn't matter," Pearce said. He un-clipped Hilda's lead. "Here," he said. "Say hello." Hilda grunted as Pearce placed him over the seats and into the back.

Kirk's eyes widened. "Fuck me," he said. "A real three-legged dog."

"Fuck me," his sister said.

"You two," Julie said. "What the fuck have I told you about swearing?"

Pearce said to Julie, "What did you want to say to me?"

She started the engine. "Mind if we don't hang around here?" she said. "The police make me nervous."

8:15 pm

Julie's daughter was called Devon – after the place where she was conceived – and Pearce found out soon enough why the kids were so fond of his dog.

"Sheba went to heaven," Devon said, out of the blue, after they'd been driving for a minute.

"Who's Sheba?" Pearce gave Julie a glance.

She was a good driver. Kept looking in the mirror like you were supposed to. A bit slow, maybe, but there was no hurry. They didn't have to be anywhere.

He still didn't know what her game was. He was curious. Couldn't help himself.

What did she want from him this time? Another £1,000 engagement ring? Well, just let her try.

They were heading out of town, along Portobello High Street.

"Sheba was our dog," Julie said in a low voice. "Border collie. Got run over. Kids were pretty fucked up about it."

"I can imagine," Pearce said. Last thing a kid needed was for their pet to die.

"Devon told you," Kirk shouted from the back. "Sheba got run over and all stuff came out of her like yucky messy goo." He paused. "Sheba went to heaven."

"She did, Kirk," Julie said, dabbing at her eye with the back of her hand. Pearce noticed her red nail polish was chipped.

"Heaven," Devon said.

Pearce sighed. He said to Julie, "I'm sorry about your dog, but that's not why you came to see me, is it?"

Julie looked in the rear-view mirror again. "There are people after me," she said.

Not very original, Pearce thought. If she was going to make up a story, she could have come up with something more inspired. Anyway, that explained why she kept looking in the mirror. Wasn't that she was a good driver, as Pearce had thought. She was looking to see if she was being followed. Or pretending that was what she was doing.

"They following you now?" Pearce asked.

"Don't see them," she said.

He said, "What do these people want with you?"

She dabbed at her eye again. Her eye-lash glistened. Her voice wobbled when she said, "Would you pass me my fags?"

She was over-doing it. Pearce saw right through it. An act. He was disappointed. She'd been doing well up till now. "I'd rather you didn't smoke," Pearce said. "Not in the car."

"Tough," she said. "It's my car."

Pearce scooped up the packet from a hollow behind the gear stick. The packet was empty. He told her.

"Fuck," she said.

Pearce played along. He was still trying to work out what the scam was. He didn't have money, so she couldn't be after that. Surely she wasn't going to ask him to borrow money from a loan shark again. He said, "So why are these people after you?"

She looked at the ring on her left hand. "Because of Mike," she said.

Pearce looked at the ring too. Not as nice as the one he'd bought her. "Your husband?" he asked.

"We're not married," she said. "Just engaged."

Even after all this time, that hurt. Pearce felt something twist inside him.

"But, yeah." Julie nodded towards the kids in the back. "He's their dad." She tapped her finger-nails on the steering wheel. Then added: "As far as I know."

"So what did their dad do that's got people following you?" Pearce asked.

"Not here," she said. "Not in front of the kids." She pulled into the kerb, un-clipped her seatbelt, opened the door. "Hang on a moment."

Pearce said, "Where you going?" but she was half-way out the door and didn't hear him. Or maybe she'd chosen to ignore him. In any case, she was gone.

So. Fine. He was alone in the car with two strange kids. Well, all kids were strange. Anyway, he was lying, it wasn't fucking fine. He'd rather have been alone in the car with a pair of mass murderers.

This wasn't Julie's scam, was it? Dump her kids on him?

No, that didn't make any sense.

She'd gone to get more fags. That was all.

At the moment, Hilda was keeping the kids happy. They were cooing and crooning, stroking his neck. And the wee fella's tongue was hanging out. He was having a grand time being the centre of attention.

Pearce might have made small talk if he'd had mass murderers in the back. But he had no idea how to make small talk with kids.

He tapped his fingertips together, peered out the window trying to work out where Julie had gone. Had to be in the newsagents. Wouldn't be long. Maybe she was working on the next part of her story.

Anyway, Pearce could handle the kids alone for a few minutes. Wasn't hard. He eyed them in the rear-view mirror, said, "Nice evening, eh?"

But they didn't reply. He liked the idea that they weren't into small talk. 'Cos neither was he. They could all just sit here and wait for their mother to return.

Hilda's growl was unexpected, 'cos it was something Pearce had rarely heard. He looked to see what was causing it. And saw Devon tugging hard on Hilda's tail.

"Stop that," Pearce said.

"Why?" Devon asked.

Pearce said, "It's hurting him."

"Why?" she asked.

"Yeah," Kirk said. "Why's it hurting?" He wiped his nose with the back of his arm.

Devon said, "Would it hurt if I had a tail?"

"That's stupid," Kirk said. "You're a stupid cunt."

Devon let go of Hilda and bawled. Instant tears. And then right before Pearce's eyes, she was sick. All over herself. And started to grin as she flicked tears out of her eyes. Lucky she'd let go of Hilda or the dog would be a spewy mess too.

Jesus fucking Christ. Where was Julie? Pearce felt hot. What if their mother had dumped them? The stench of sick floated from the back and he thought he might throw up too. He'd cleaned up plenty of dog puke in his time, but human puke was a different story.

He opened his window. Leaned out. Caught a glimpse of Julie coming out of the shop about fifteen feet away, looking around her as if she was trying to spot someone she knew.

She hadn't run off. Thank Christ.

Pearce realised the kids were being very quiet. Turned to look in the back. Hilda was lapping away at the girl's puke.

Jesus.

He reached into the back, grabbed Hilda and lifted him into the front. The dog wasn't happy. Pushed against him, wanting to get back to the food source.

Kirk said, "Your dog eats sick."

Then Julie opened her door. "What's that stink?"

Pearce quickly explained about the puking incident. Asked if Julie had something to clean it up with.

Julie said, "Didn't your dog want it?"

8:30 pm

Julie found some wet wipes in the glove box and cleaned up the rest of Devon's puke. After she'd mopped up as best she could, Pearce said, "Are you going to finish your story?"

Julie sniffed her fingers, lit a cigarette. "Where was I?"

"You were telling me about your boyfriend, Mike," Pearce said.

Julie started the car. Pulled out without indicating. "Mike, yeah," she said. "So I was."

"What did he do?" Pearce asked.

"Daddy!" Kirk said. "Where's Daddy?"

"Keep your voice down," Julie said to Pearce.

"So what happened?" he whispered to her. He was keen to hear what tales she was going to spin him. "Did Mike kill someone?" he asked.

"Daddy!" Devon said. "Bollocks!"

"Shut the fuck up," Julie said to the kids. To Pearce she said, quietly, "No, he didn't kill anyone."

"That's good," Pearce said, stroking Hilda's chin.

Julie banged her fist on the steering wheel, made Hilda jump. "It's not."

He looked at her. "You wanted him to kill someone?"

"Not me," she said. "Banksy wanted him to kill someone."

35

"Who's Banksy?" Pearce asked.

"You know," she said. "The loan shark."

Pearce thought for a minute. "You mean Kevin Banks? He's moved up?"

"Yeah." She took a deep breath. "Calls himself Banksy now," she said.

For a very short time Pearce had worked for a loan shark called Cooper. This guy, Banksy, had also worked for Cooper as a collector. Only back then he was known plain and simple as Kevin Banks. Must have branched out on his own after Cooper was sent to prison.

"Mike owed Banksy money? Banksy wanted someone dead?" Pearce said. "I'm confused. You want to start at the beginning?"

"Banksy's more than just a loan shark," Julie said. "At least, he thinks so. Sees himself as Leith's answer to Tony Soprano. Dabbles in anything and everything that makes money, as long as it's not legit. Small crew. Main players are Banksy and two other guys: his brother Ray and an older guy called Jack." She paused. "Jack Bower."

Pearce waited.

"It's real," she said. "It's his real name."

Pearce shrugged. No reason it shouldn't be.

Julie went on, "Banksy has his slimy fingers in everything." She breathed out sharply. "Mike owed him big time."

"How much?" Pearce asked.

"Twenty grand," she said.

"That's enough," Pearce said. Julie's story was getting better. He was enjoying it. She'd worked hard on making it convincing. She'd managed to involve Banksy, which was very clever. The time Pearce worked for Cooper was the same time Julie was on the scene. He was impressed. "I'm guessing a lot of that twenty grand was interest?" he said.

"You bet," she said, her voice quieter. "Anyway, Mike lost his job about six months ago. Landlord said he'd evict us. The bank wouldn't lend Mike any money. So he borrowed a few grand to tide us over till he got a new job. But days passed, and weeks passed, and months passed, and still no sign of a job. And meanwhile the interest grew. Got out of control."

She took a long drag, made her cheek-bones stick out. "In the end, Banksy wouldn't wait any longer. Said he wanted his money back. All of it. Right away. And Mike had no means of getting it."

Pearce thought he could see where this was going. Mike was going to get an arm or a leg broken. Something like that.

Julie said, "Can I trust you, Pearce?"

Pearce sat up. The cheek of the woman was amazing. If anyone should be asking that question, he should be asking her. "I don't know," he said.

She shook her head. "I suppose not. But I have to. Look, what I did to you was terrible and I'm sorry. I needed the cash and I used you to get it. But I did honestly like you."

Fuck's sake, was that supposed to be an apology?

"I've paid attention to what you've been up to," she said. "Heard all about your mum, of course. Tragic, her death."

"Long time ago," Pearce said.

Julie said, "And I saw all that in the papers about you rescuing some crazy guy who'd been held captive in a cage. That sounded weird."

Pearce had a flashback to being tied to a bench in a stinking basement. He didn't want to think about that. It had taken a while but he was over it now. He said, "I didn't exactly rescue him."

"Oh," she said. "Well, can't trust the papers, eh? Anyway, it doesn't matter. The point is, I haven't forgotten you. Look, Pearce, I don't know who else I can turn to."

Pearce nearly laughed but managed to stop himself. Julie thought she was playing him for a sucker. Let her. He had no idea where this was leading, but he was going to hear her out, just for the fun of telling her he'd seen through it and pointing out exactly where she could shove it.

"What about Mike?" Pearce asked.

Julie lit another fag from the stub of the one she was finishing. She had trouble doing so. Her hand was shaking. Pearce waited for her to go on. After a few drags she said, "Do you know what a kill clock is, Pearce?"

He'd never heard of it. He told her so.

She said, "I'll pull over. I don't want to talk about this in front of the kids."

8:45 pm

They were standing outside the car, leaning on the bonnet. Pearce had let Hilda into the back once more. The dog and the kids were keeping each other amused. Devon waved. Pearce waved back.

Julie flicked her cigarette away. Licked her lips. She said, "A kill clock's what it's called when you have to murder someone within a set time."

"What," Pearce said, "like you get an hour to kill someone?"

"Often longer," she said. "Twenty-four hours. So you can prepare. Work out how best to do it. So you have a slight chance of getting away with it."

"Mike got one of these ... kill clocks?" Pearce asked.

"Yeah," she said. "There's a guy Banksy really wanted out of the way."

"Why couldn't Banksy get rid of the guy himself?" Pearce wanted to know.

Her voice cracked. "No idea. Didn't want to get his hands dirty, I suppose." Her hands were shaking so badly she burned her fingers as she took another drag of her cigarette. "Fuck," she said as she dropped it. She shook her hand, blew on her fingers.

"You OK?" Pearce asked.

She nodded. "Anyway," she said, "Banksy gave Mike twenty-four hours to kill this guy."

Pearce said, "And wipe out his debt? Twenty grand for a hit. That's good pay." Pearce didn't know if that was true. But he wanted to see how Julie responded. "Professional rates," he added.

"Banksy wasn't going to let Mike off the hook that lightly," she said. "But it was going to be a start. Pay off a big chunk. Leave an amount we could manage."

Pearce nodded. She was pretty good at thinking fast on her feet. "Did Mike do it?" he asked.

She shook her head. Stared up the road. They were parked off the main road in a quiet side street. There wasn't much to stare at. She looked back at him.

"He tried," she said. "Mike's dead, Pearce."

The story was getting even more elaborate. Pearce was impressed once again. All the hand-trembling made it seem real.

Even now, there was a tear in her eye as she spoke.

Nice act. He felt like clapping.

"How did that happen?" Pearce asked. "How did he die?"

She looked down at the road. "The guy Mike was supposed to kill? He killed Mike instead."

Pearce cleared his throat. "You've been to the police?"

"Yeah," she said.

"And what did they say?" he asked.

She said, "They didn't believe me."

Pearce said, "Why not?"

"They think Mike's done a runner," she told him.

"What about the body?" he asked.

"There isn't one," she said. "The guy Mike was supposed to kill sent his body back to Banksy."

Pearce was silent for a moment. "Well, maybe Mike *has* done a runner?"

She shook her head.

"How can you be so sure?" he asked her.

"Banksy showed me a picture ... of ... of Mike," she said. "It wasn't pretty."

"What did they do with ... the body?" Pearce asked.

"I don't know," she said. "Got rid of it."

She looked as if she were about to burst into tears.

"When did this happen?" Pearce asked.

"Day before yesterday," she said.

"I'm sorry," Pearce said, growing ever more impressed by her acting. She did look upset. "But why have you come to me?"

"Because I need help," she said.

"Go to the police," he said. "Tell them what you've told me."

"I have," she said.

"And?" he asked.

"They don't believe me," she said.

He said, "It's a hell of a story, right enough."

"Not helped by the fact that they think I'm a nut-job," she said.

"They do?" Pearce asked.

"I've spent some time in the Royal Edinburgh," she said. "My head got fucked up, you know."

"Right," Pearce said. He hadn't known that, but he didn't think it was a lie. If anything had the ring of truth about it, that did. "That's not going to help. Look, what can I do for you?" He crossed his arms. It was cool but dry. The earlier drizzle hadn't come to anything. "It's over," he said. "Mike's dead. The debt is written off. End of story. No?"

"I wish it was, Pearce." She looked at him. "Banksy still wants his money. He says it's down to me now. And he gave me twenty-four hours to pay it back."

"When's that up?" Pearce said.

She looked at her watch. "Fifty minutes ago."

Pearce pushed himself off the bonnet. "So where is he?"

"I was careful," she said. "He'll have to find me."

Pearce said, "I don't see how I can help."

"I just want you to talk to him for me," she said. "You know him."

"I don't," he said.

She said, "But you worked with him."

47

"Nope," he told her. "I knew of him but the only guy I worked with apart from Cooper was called Joe Hope."

"But you know people Banksy knows," she said. "You can talk to him. You have to, Pearce. Get him to let me pay him back over time. I'll pay it all back. I will. Honest. I just can't do it all at once. I don't have the money."

"Why don't you ask him yourself?" Pearce suggested.

"He won't listen to me. He says me and Mike already had too many chances."

"I really don't think I can help," Pearce said.

Julie said, "Have a fucking heart."

9:00 pm

"I'm baffled, Julie," Pearce said. "Why do you think I'd agree to help you? Last time I saw you, you ripped me off. You don't get in touch for years. Then you swing on by as if we're best friends, spinning some crazy tale about your dead boyfriend and a loan shark. Well, you know what? I'm not falling for it."

She stared at him and said, "You don't believe me?"

"Dead fucking right," he said.

"Oh, God," she said. "I never thought … You have to believe me. Every fucking word is true."

Pearce said, "Well, I don't, no matter how much you fucking swear."

She opened the car, took out her bag. Rummaged around in it, found her mobile. She said, "Call Banksy. Ask him."

"Oh," Pearce said. "So he's in on the scam too, is he?"

She thrust her mobile at him.

He backed off. "I'm not calling anyone."

A passing car inched past. Then stopped. Sat with the engine running.

For a moment, Pearce thought it was just someone who'd got lost. But then he noticed the driver was wearing a ski mask.

Car doors clicked open. Two guys got out. They were wearing ski masks too. The driver stayed put.

Julie was frozen to the spot. She dropped her phone.

Nice touch, Pearce thought. He folded his arms, watched the drama unfold.

One of the guys grabbed Julie.

She screamed, "Help me, Pearce! Help me!"

He looked in Julie's car, saw the kids staring out, terrified at what was happening to their mother. He couldn't believe she'd put her kids through this. They believed what they were seeing was for real. Their mother was a bitch.

"Stop this shite," he said. "You're scaring the kids."

One of the masked men had Julie in a firm hold round her waist, arms pinned to her sides. He lifted her off the ground. She stopped screaming while she tried to kick him.

51

The other man pointed a gun at Pearce. It was fitted with a silencer. Probably stuck that on to hide the fact it was a fancy water pistol. They might think they were fooling Pearce, but he wasn't so easily fucking fooled these days.

Pearce put his hands up and said in a pretend scared voice, "Don't shoot. Please don't shoot."

Julie yelled something about her babies, so maybe the gunman didn't hear him. His partner had carried Julie to the car. Rear door was open. He tried to shove her inside. She wasn't making it easy.

All very dramatic, but Pearce had just about had enough. "Very good," he said. "But it's just not going to work."

The gunman pointed the gun at Pearce again. "Shut your fucking mouth," he said.

"You can drop the act now," Pearce said.

"I told you to shut it, pal," the gunman said.

The other masked man was still struggling with Julie. She was half in, half out of the car, kicking and yelling. She'd lost a shoe in the struggle.

"What're you going to do if I don't?" Pearce said to the guy who'd told him to shut it. "Shoot me?"

The gunman pulled the trigger. There was a dull sound, then something ricocheted off the road beside Pearce's foot, leaving a ragged hole in the tarmac. Pearce jumped backwards. He couldn't help himself. He'd been shot twice and didn't fancy it again.

These guys were serious. A con was a con, but this was taking things too far. If they were using real guns, someone could easily get hurt. He couldn't believe that Julie would have OK'd this. Not with her kids on hand.

He looked towards her. She'd stopped struggling. Maybe the gun-shot had been her signal to be quiet. Or maybe she really had been scared into silence. She'd been slid into the back seat, one of the masked men between her and the door.

The other one, the one with the gun, spoke to Pearce. "You listening?"

Pearce said, "You listen."

"You're courting death, pal," the gunman said.

"Julie?" Pearce said. "Are you OK?"

She didn't say anything. Maybe because the guy in the back seat had his hand clamped over her mouth.

"Hey, pal," the gunman said to Pearce. "Get your eyes off her. Look over here."

Pearce looked at him.

"Here's the deal," the gunman said. "Go to the police and your girlfriend's dead."

"She's not my girlfriend," Pearce said.

"She'll still be dead," he said. "Got it?"

Pearce nodded.

"But if you bring Banksy twenty grand by midnight," the gunman said, "she can go free."

"I don't have twenty grand," Pearce said.

"Then she's dead," the gunman said.

"I don't have twenty grand," Pearce repeated.

"A clever guy like you," the gunman said. "I'm sure you can find it."

Pearce said nothing.

"Twenty grand," the gunman repeated. "By midnight." He kicked Julie's mobile phone across the tarmac towards Pearce. "Banksy will be in touch."

Panic Time
9:10 pm

Pearce picked up the phone, watched them drive away. Julie's shoe lay on its side in the road. He walked over to it, picked it up.

He turned towards Julie's car. Kirk and Devon were staring out the window at him.

This was going to be hard to explain.

He got in. Driver's side. Hilda jumped onto his lap. The car smelt faintly of sick. He opened the window.

"Where's Mummy gone?" Kirk said.

"She's had to go away," Pearce told him.

Kirk said, "That man had a gun."

"He did," Pearce replied.

"My heart was beating," Kirk said. "Faster and faster."

"Faster," Devon said.

"Shut up, you cunt," Kirk told her.

Pearce said, "Watch the language."

"They had funny faces," Devon said.

"I don't want Mummy to go," Kirk said.

"Neither do I, Kirk." Pearce started the engine. "But what are we going to do about it?

Kirk said, "I don't want her to go."

"Me neither," Pearce said.

Kirk said, "I don't like you."

"I don't like you, too," Devon said.

Pearce looked in the rear-view mirror. Devon was grinning. Kirk wasn't, the little bastard.

Kirk said, "Give me Mummy's shoe."

Pearce gave it to him.

He started to wail.

Pearce said, "It's OK. Kirk?"

Kirk wailed louder.

"Hey," Pearce said. "It's OK, son."

Kirk wailed louder.

Only one thing for it. Pearce turned on the radio. He turned up the volume till he drowned out Kirk. Which was hard. Because Kirk was screaming now, and Devon had joined in, still grinning.

Pearce hummed along to the music. Tapped his fingers on the steering wheel. He was getting the hang of driving again. All clicked back into place.

But he could use a bit of quiet to help him focus. He had things to work out. Like, where the fuck was he going? He'd swung round, and without thinking about it was headed back home. He knew all too well that at the moment all he was doing was driving someone else's car with someone else's kids in the back. If he was stopped, it wouldn't look too good. Maybe he should own up. Go to the nearest police station.

There was one in Portobello. He could explain what had happened. The kids could back him up. If Kirk ever shut the fuck up, wailing little fucker. But the gunman had said that if Pearce went to the police, they'd kill Julie. That wasn't Pearce's problem, but he couldn't do that to the kids. They weren't to blame for the mess their mother had got herself in.

So he couldn't go to the police. Which was a shame. That would have solved everything.

Jesus. Pearce could have sworn it was all a con. Right up until the moment that guy had fired at him. Or rather, fired at the ground.

Hell, he still wasn't totally sure that what he'd just seen was real. There was still a chance that it was a con.

Back then, Pearce had only known Julie for two weeks before he got engaged to her. Far too soon, yeah. He knew that. But it had seemed right at the time. Point was, would Julie have left someone like him to look after her kids?

Pearce thought she might. If the money was right.

And that's where the solution lay. Pearce's lack of money. If you were to go to such lengths to rip someone off, you'd make sure they had something worth ripping off in the first place. And Pearce didn't.

So he had to assume that it was real.

Julie had been kidnapped. She was going to die if he didn't find twenty grand by midnight.

He didn't fucking believe it. But he had to.

What was he going to do?

First thing: get the kids somewhere safe. That was easier said than done. He didn't know anyone who'd be happy to look after a couple of pre-school kids. Didn't know that many people at all. But he had to dump the kids before he could go and look for their mother. They weren't safe with all these bullets flying around. Apart from which, it had to be way past their bedtime.

Seeing Julie again had triggered all sorts of memories from that time six years ago. Some good, some not so good. One of the good ones was Ailsa. He hadn't seen her since then. But she'd helped Pearce out back then. Got him hooked up with a gun runner when he'd needed a weapon. And he couldn't think of anywhere else to go.

He just had to hope that Ailsa hadn't moved house since he'd last paid her a visit.

9:30 pm

Couldn't park near Ailsa's flat on Easter Road so he had to find a slot in a nearby side street. During the drive over, Kirk had finally shut up. And when he shut up, so did his sister.

Pearce hadn't been able to find a station he wanted to listen to and spent most of the journey twiddling the dial on the radio.

After a few near-accidents, he'd given up. Left it on some Scottish fiddle music station. The music was doing his head in more than their yelling had done. But he'd made his point.

When they finally shut up, he was able to turn off the radio.

Five minutes of relative quiet before Kirk said, "Where are we?"

Pearce found a space big enough for him to park on Rossie Place. There were smaller spaces nearby, but he didn't fancy his chances of parking without causing some damage. Parking had never been his strong point.

"We're going to see a nice lady," Pearce said.

Kirk asked him, "Where's Mummy?"

"Mummy!" Devon said. She held out Julie's shoe.

"The nice lady's called Ailsa," Pearce said.

Kirk said, "Is she your girlfriend?"

"No," Pearce said, shutting off the engine.

"Are you gay?" Kirk asked.

Pearce closed his eyes. How anyone could put up with this constant irritation was beyond belief.

"Gay," Devon said. "You're gay."

Pearce had a good mind to leave them in the car. Just while he went to see Ailsa. They'd be fine. What was the alternative? Drag them out of the car, kicking and screaming? Yeah, he'd fetch Ailsa. She'd be able to get them to go with her much more easily.

"I have to pop out for a moment," he said. Hilda wagged his tail. "Will you two be good till I get back?"

"Don't leave me!" Kirk said. "No!"

"You sure you don't want to stay?" Pearce asked. "After all, you don't like me and I'm gay."

"I do," Devon said. "I like you. You're funny."

"No," Kirk said. "It's dark."

"You're afraid of the dark?" Pearce said. "A big boy like you?"

"No," Devon said.

Kirk said, "Yeah."

"That's a bit gay," Pearce said.

"Is not," Kirk said.

"That's OK," Pearce said. "Nothing wrong with being gay."

Kirk said, "I want to see your girlfriend."

"You ever listen?" Pearce said. "She's not my girlfriend."

"You're gay," Devon said.

"Devon," Pearce said. "Do you know what that means?"

Devon beamed at him and shook her head.

"You want to come too?" he asked her.

"Hilda!" she yelled.

"You should be tired," he said.

"Yes!" she said. "Tired!"

"Yeah," Pearce told her. "Come on, then. We can all go. One big happy fucking family."

9:45 pm

He rang Ailsa's buzzer. Her name was still on the name-plate, which was a good sign. He'd had to let go of Kirk's hand but the kid didn't look in any danger of running away. He was too scared. Had been since Pearce said he might leave him in the car. Kirk clung to Pearce's side. Pearce patted him on the head.

"Hello?" Ailsa's voice.

And with it, a whole bunch of thoughts and images rose in Pearce's mind. Sorting out her violent boyfriend. Cooking breakfast in her kitchen. Buying a gun from a fat bloke with a Mohican hair-cut. A friend of hers. Getting shot with the same gun. Waking up in hospital. Telling her to go away, to leave him alone. It would never work.

"Pearce," he said.

"Who?" she said.

He moved closer to the speaker. "Pearce."

"Pearce," she said. "Pearce? Jesus Christ."

The door buzzed.

He pushed it open, held it for Kirk and Devon. Kirk handed Hilda's lead back to him. Devon gave him her fairy wand and her mum's shoe.

They trooped along to Ailsa's flat. Pearce was about to ring the bell when the door opened.

"Pearce," Ailsa said, face bright, hardly aged at all, looking great. Then she saw Kirk and Devon and her expression changed. She said, "What's going on?"

"Well," he said, stuffing the fairy wand in his armpit, holding Julie's shoe out as if it explained everything. "Remember I used to have a girlfriend, Julie? These are her kids. Kirk and Devon." Then, to the kids he said, "Say hi to Ailsa."

Kirk scowled.

Devon said, "Bollocks."

Pearce said, "These two have lost their mother."

"And?" Ailsa said.

"I was hoping you could look after them till I find her," he said.

Ailsa turned round, closed the door.

Pearce stood there and stared at it. He looked at the kids. They looked back at him. He stared at the door. They stared at it, too.

No amount of staring made any difference. It stayed closed.

Devon leaned up, pointed to the fairy wand. He gave it to her. She waved it. "Bradabra," she said.

Nothing.

"Thanks for trying," Pearce said. He rang the bell again.

No more effective than Devon's wand.

He rang it again.

Ailsa opened the door, said, "You come here after all these years expecting me to look after your girlfriend's children?"

"Julie's not my girlfriend," he said.

"Go away, Pearce," she said.

She closed the door again.

Devon put her arm round his leg. "It's OK," she said, looking up at him.

10:00 pm

Back in the car, Pearce said, "What are we going to do with you two?"

Kirk said, "I want to go home."

"Can't do that, Kirk," Pearce said. "There's no-one at home to look after you."

"Daddy," Devon said.

Pearce breathed through his nose. "I don't think so."

"Where is he?" Kirk said.

"You don't know?" Pearce said.

"Mummy said he'd gone away."

Jesus. Julie hadn't told them Mike was dead. Unless this was part of the scam, too. Maybe Mike was sitting at home grinning away to himself right now, wondering how Pearce was coping with his kids.

Kirk said, "Can we go to your home?"

"Can't leave you there either, Kirk," Pearce said. "I have to go out. Find your mum."

"Is she lost?" Kirk asked.

"No," Pearce said. "I know where she is." He started the engine.

Devon said, "Granny's."

"Granny's?" Pearce said.

"Mummy's at Granny's," she said.

"Don't know about that," Pearce said. "But do you want to go to Granny's?"

"Yeah," Devon said. "Hilda wants to go to Granny's too."

Pearce asked, "I don't suppose you know where Granny lives?"

10:05 pm

They didn't know where Granny lived, but her number was stored on Julie's mobile.

Pearce called her, quickly explained that he was a friend of Julie's, that he had her grand-children and wasn't sure what to do with them.

She wanted to know where Julie was.

He said Julie had had to go somewhere in a hurry.

She wanted to know where her son was.

"Your son?" Pearce asked.

"Mike," she said. "Julie's boyfriend."

Fuck, Pearce had taken it for granted that she was Julie's mother. He'd also thought that Julie would have told her about her son being killed. Hadn't told anyone shit. Apart from Pearce. Unless this was a scam, of course, in which case Mike was alive and well and it was no surprise that neither his kids nor his mother had heard of his death 'cos he wasn't fucking dead.

"I don't know," Pearce said. "How do I get to your place?"

Granny told him where she lived. It wasn't far. Which was good. Pearce wasn't enjoying driving. It wouldn't have been so bad if he'd been alone in the car but he didn't like being in charge of the young passengers in the back.

On the way to Granny's, the kids fell asleep, so Pearce had a moment to consider what he was going to do after he'd dropped them off.

Maybe it was a scam. Maybe. He just wasn't sure. It hadn't sounded like the truth when Julie was telling Pearce what happened to her boyfriend, despite the tear in her eye, but she'd made up for it when she'd been kidnapped.

If she hadn't ripped him off before, he wouldn't have any doubts.

He had to believe it was real, though. For the kids.

So, what was he to do?

He didn't have the means to raise twenty grand to free Julie – and that was even supposing Banksy would let her go. She knew too much. Of course, the same thing could be said of Pearce. Maybe Banksy wouldn't let him live either.

Which meant that Pearce had to consider how best to protect himself.

He called 118118 and asked for Ailsa's home number.

When she answered, he said, "Don't hang up." Before she could reply, he said, "Never mind the kids. I've found out where their granny lives. They'll be fine. I don't need your help with them. But I do need your help with something else."

A long pause. He listened to the hum of the car engine, watched a young couple shouting at each other on the pavement, prayed Ailsa wouldn't hang up.

She didn't. She said, "You can't just walk back into my life like this."

"I'm not," Pearce said. "I just need your help this one time. Then I'm gone."

"Christ," Ailsa said. "That's no fucking better. You're as hopeless as ever."

"Does that mean you'll help?" he asked.

Another pause. Then, "What is it you want?" she said.

"You still in touch with that fat bloke with the Mohican hair-cut?" Pearce asked.

"His name's Joe-Bob," she said.

"That's the guy," Pearce said. "Well, are you?"

Ailsa said, "You after what I think you're after?"

"Please," he said. Joe-Bob sold guns.

"Jesus, Pearce," she said. "Look what happened last time you got a ... you know."

She didn't want to say the word on the phone. Smart. "I know," he said. "But this time I'll be careful."

"I dunno," she said.

"I need it tonight," Pearce said. "As soon as possible. If you can't do it, I need to know. Make other plans."

She sighed. "God knows why I'm doing this," she said. "Call me back in half an hour."

"Something powerful," he said. "That'll fit in a tool-bag. I need to look like I mean it."

When he arrived at the kids' granny's, she was waiting by the kerb-side. She was in her early fifties, slim, fit-looking, still a good-looking woman, not the saggy-titted bingo-winged old dear Pearce had pictured.

He didn't know it was her till she stepped towards the car. He opened the door and she said, "You must be Pearce. I tried phoning Mike. Tried him at home, tried his mobile. No answer. You sure you don't know where he is?"

Pearce thought about telling her, but Kirk woke up and saw Granny and started to tell her all about the guns and the masked men. He rescued Julie's shoe from where it had fallen onto the floor and showed it to his granny.

Even in the dark, Pearce could see Granny's face pale. Pearce decided to keep quiet about Mike. He shouldn't be the one to have to tell her about her son. And, anyway, he couldn't be sure that Mike was dead.

Granny invited Pearce in. He nodded, said he had to be quick.

They carried one kid each up the steps to her first floor flat.

Devon snuggled close to Pearce's chest. She took her thumb out of her mouth for long enough to say, "Cold."

"It'll be warm in Granny's," Pearce said.

And it was. Granny liked her heating turned up.

The kids plunked themselves down in front of the TV whilst Granny went off to make them a milky drink. "Come with me," she said to Pearce.

Pearce went with her into the kitchen.

"What happened to Julie?" Granny asked him. "What was Kirk talking about?"

Maybe he couldn't tell her about Mike. But he had to tell her what had happened to Julie. Kirk's account had been a mess. Pearce had to see if he could do better.

He explained it to Granny as quickly and matter-of-factly as he could.

"Why didn't you tell me on the phone?" she said.

Pearce said, "It's easier face to face."

"Oh, Lord," she said. "We need to call the police."

"No," he said. "We need to wait. I'll sort things out. I'm meeting the guy who kidnapped her, Banksy, at midnight."

"Banksy?" she said. She looked down at her hand. "Oh, Lord."

"You know him?" Pearce said. He followed her gaze. He hadn't seen it before. The top half of the little finger of her left hand was missing. The stump was smooth. "Banksy did that?" Pearce asked.

She nodded, closing her eyes – she must have been remembering the pain of it. "I wouldn't have thought it was possible. Banksy and his brother, Ray, wondered too." She opened her eyes, looked at the finger. "They did it here. In the sitting room. Ray waited by the open door while Banksy got my hand in a grip like this."

She showed Pearce, clasping her hands round his, holding out the little finger, keeping it bent back and straight.

"Pushed it into the space between the door frame and the edge of the door." She paused. "Then Ray slammed it shut." She shuddered, stroked the tip of Pearce's pinkie. "Snapped clean through the bone."

"Fuck." Pearce pulled his hand away. "Couldn't they stick it back on at the hospital?"

"Maybe," she said. "But those bastards took that part of my finger away with them."

Pearce said, "How much did you owe them?"

"I didn't owe them anything," she said. "Mike did."

"When was this?" Pearce asked.

"Long time ago," she said. "Three years or so now."

More evidence to support Julie's claim that Mike owed money. "He's been in debt before, then," Pearce said.

"He's in debt again?" Granny said. "Oh, Lord."

"I'm afraid so," Pearce said. "That's why they've got Julie."

"I'm worried about him, Pearce," she said.

And rightly so. If he was going to tell her her son was dead, now would be the time. But he couldn't. He didn't have the heart. But he couldn't lie to her either, tell her everything would be OK. Instead, he patted her hand and got up.

Devon appeared in the doorway, wand in hand, wearing her mother's shoe. "Where's my drink?" she said.

10:45 pm

Outside, it felt chilly after the heat of Granny's flat. But Pearce warmed up when it struck him that Julie's car was gone.

He didn't mind walking. Never had a problem with that.

What he minded was that he'd left Hilda in the car.

He didn't have much time to think about his missing dog, though, 'cos at that moment, Julie's phone rang.

"Pearce?" a man's voice said. "I've heard all about you."

"Like-wise, Banksy," Pearce said. It had to be Banksy. Who else would be calling him on Julie's mobile?

"Hope nobody's been saying anything bad about me." Banksy chuckled. "It's all lies, you know."

Pearce said, "Let Julie go."

"I will," he said. "Of course. But only if you bring my money to me by midnight."

"I don't have twenty grand," Pearce said.

"Guy like you, Pearce," Banksy said, "I find it hard to believe that you don't have a big pile of cash stashed away somewhere."

Pearce said, "If I did, I wouldn't give it to you."

"Is that right?" Banksy said.

Pearce heard muffled voices as Banksy moved away from the phone. When Banksy came back, it was to say, "Listen to this. Maybe you'll change your mind."

And then there was an almighty scream. A woman's scream. It went on and on and on. If she was acting, it was damn good acting.

Banksy spoke again. "You already have deaths on your conscience, Pearce. You think you can stand one more? Maybe you can. That's fine. It's up to you."

At one point, the easy option for Pearce would have been to walk away from this whole thing. Ignore it. It wasn't his problem. The kids were with their granny. She could look after them.

But Pearce was involved now, whether he wanted to be or not. Banksy had taken his dog.

Pearce breathed deeply. "Where?"

Banksy said, "What?" as if he hadn't been listening.

"Where should I take the money?"

"Ah, that's more like it," Banksy said. "And we'll make it nice and easy for you."

Banksy told Pearce they'd meet him at a trading estate less than five minutes from where he lived. Pearce knew exactly where Banksy meant. He saw it every day from his sitting room window.

But why the fuck were they coming to Pearce's turf? Leith, Banksy's patch, was only a stone's throw away. He had to ask. "You're coming to me?" he said.

"Sure," Banksy said. "We like to be helpful, you know." Then, in a more sinister tone, "Listen, we know where you live."

So that was it, Pearce thought. They wanted to rub in the fact that he couldn't hide from them.

"If you don't bring the money," Banksy said, "we'll dump Julie on your door-step. One piece at a time. Got that?"

"Yeah," Pearce said. It was worse than he'd thought. "I've got that."

"And before you go," Banksy said. "Someone else wants to say hi."

Pearce listened. Heard a yelp. Sounded like a dog.

Fuck. "Hilda?" Pearce said. "Leave him the fuck alone."

"You of all people should know better than to leave your dog where it's not safe," Banksy said. "I hear you're very fond of it. Don't understand the appeal myself. It's a vile-looking thing. And it stinks of vomit."

Hilda had been stolen once before. Sounded like Banksy had done his homework. Well, it wasn't all bad. The car hadn't been stolen by joy-riders, so at least Pearce knew where Hilda was.

"Fuck you," Pearce said.

"Oh," Banksy said, and blew a kiss down the line. Then it went dead.

11:00 pm

Pearce flagged down a taxi. Once he was seated, he called Ailsa.

"Did you speak to Joe-Bob?" he asked.

"He'll meet you tonight," she said.

"With ..." Pearce almost said, 'the gun', but remembered he was on a mobile phone just in time. "With ... something powerful?"

"Yeah," she said. "Very. Just say when and where."

Pearce asked, "Can I speak to him?"

"Make your plans through me," she said.

Pearce thought for a moment. "Make it 11:30," he said. "Foot of King's Road. There are some benches that look out across the Firth of Forth. I'll be sitting on one of them."

For a moment he wondered if the police might still be around from the earlier incident when he'd smashed up that slap-head fuck's car. But it would have been taken away by now. The police would be long gone. It'd be safe enough.

"I'll tell him," she said.

"How much?" Pearce asked.

"He's not a plumber," she said. "He doesn't normally do emergency call-outs. And he's not too fond of you."

Pearce and Joe-Bob's one and only previous meeting hadn't gone too well. Point was, Ailsa was telling Pearce that the gun wasn't going to come cheap. "Well?" he asked.

She told him.

"Ah," he said.

"Is that a problem?" she asked.

"I can't afford it," he said. "Not even close."

"You want to rent it instead of buy it?" she suggested.

"I can do that?" he said.

"I'll get back to you," she said, and hung up.

The taxi driver tried chatting to him for a while. Pearce just grunted yes or no as seemed appropriate while he waited for Ailsa to call back. The driver soon got the message that Pearce wasn't much of a talker.

Ailsa called back within five minutes. "Joe-Bob said that's fine," she said. "For five hundred quid you get to use it for twenty-four hours," she told him. "Return it to Joe-Bob when you're finished."

"Sounds good," Pearce said. "I won't need it after tonight."

After he hung up, he stared out the window, let his mind drift. The threat of a gun alone wouldn't be enough. Banksy and his crew were armed – they'd shown that when they kidnapped Julie. Whatever weapon Joe-Bob came up with, Pearce would have to be ready to use it. Which in turn meant he'd have to be ready to take the consequences. Killing someone. Going to jail. Again.

Yeah, he'd much prefer to walk away. Julie was nothing to him. For a long time, he'd hated her. Hated the fact she'd made him look such a fool by fucking off with the engagement ring. If this had all happened a few years ago, he'd have left her to rot. But his anger had faded over the years. Until he'd forgotten her.

But now she was back. Not playing an elaborate con on him, as he'd thought. Well, it didn't look that way. She was asking for his help.

Well, fuck her, anyway. He wasn't doing this for her. He'd make sure she knew that.

He was doing this because Banksy had made it personal, stealing his fucking dog. And, well, maybe because Julie's kids needed their mother.

His phone rang. Ailsa again. "Joe-Bob wants to meet a bit later," she said. "Is 11:45 OK?"

"Yeah," Pearce said. "But he can't afford to be late. Make sure he knows that someone's life's at stake."

"Will do," she said. "See you later."

11:20 pm

Back home, Pearce grabbed a tool bag from the top shelf. Got covered in dust as he took it down. Wiped it off with a towel. Wondered if he should get some magazines and newspapers, cut them into strips, band them together like they do in the movies.

See, Pearce didn't have the twenty grand to ransom Julie, so he was going to have to pretend he did.

But he couldn't see the point of bundling up strips of newspaper into stacks. It wouldn't take a genius to see that it wasn't real money. Even if he put some real notes on top, first thing Banksy would do was flip through a stack, see if the rest were genuine or not.

Apart from which, Pearce didn't have time to waste cutting up newspapers. He'd have to make do with loading the bag with a few library books. Had to leave room for the gun, though.

On the way home, he'd asked the taxi to stop while he got some cash out of a machine with his bank card. Had to take out some more with his credit card to make up the five hundred.

When he'd got back, he'd half expected the police to be waiting for him to question him about crashing that slap-head's car. But there was no-one around. And when he walked in the door, Hilda wasn't there to greet him.

Still, he didn't have long to worry about that. He'd get Hilda back soon.

The clock was ticking.

He put on a black jumper, slipped on a pair of leather gloves, grabbed the bag. He'd get down to the beach early, wait for Joe-Bob to arrive. No point sitting here twiddling his thumbs when he could twiddle his thumbs out in the fresh air.

11:30 pm

There was no sign of the car. Glass still lay on the road, though, from where he'd smashed the wind-screen. He could see it sparkle in the light of a street-lamp.

Behind Pearce, the bar was closed. Early, Pearce thought. But maybe not. He wasn't sure what time pubs closed during the week. He rarely set foot in them. He didn't drink much. When he did, it was at home. He didn't like pubs. They tended to be full of pissed people, and he found pissed people tiring.

Pearce sat on one of the metal benches over-looking the beach, the cold hitting the backs of his thighs through his jeans. To the west, clusters of lights twinkled on the coast. Closer, on an island in the Forth, a light-house flashed every few seconds. In the distance the lights of a distant oil-rig or maybe a tanker glowed. Waves churned up a background white noise.

Very restful.

He closed his eyes.

11:43 pm

"Pearce?"

Pearce opened his eyes. Joe-Bob was thinner than Pearce remembered. You still wouldn't describe him as slim, but he was in better shape than he'd been six years ago. Still had the Mohican hair-cut, although Pearce couldn't tell by the light of the street-lamp if he still dyed it red. Everything was tinted orange.

Joe-Bob slid off his back-pack, placed it next to Pearce on the bench. He held out his hand.

Pearce ignored it.

Joe-Bob shook his head. "Still a rude cunt, eh?" he said.

"Still a fat fuck?" Pearce said. That'd hurt. But Pearce didn't want to be nice to this guy. He was a drug dealer. Well, once upon a time. Now he dealt in illegal weapons.

"You shouldn't talk to people like that," Joe-Bob said. "Not when they're armed."

"Just give me the fucking gun," Pearce said.

Joe-Bob said, "Just trying to be polite."

Pearce said, "Give me the fucking gun."

Joe-Bob looked at him. Then he unzipped his bag. "Powerful enough for you?" he said.

Pearce took a look. He didn't know shit about guns, but it looked like a small machine gun, the sort you'd see in action movies and video games. "What is it?" he asked.

"Mini Uzi," Joe-Bob said.

"That's powerful, is it?" Pearce asked.

Joe-Bob gave him that look again. Made Pearce want to smack him. Joe-Bob said, "Sixteen rounds per second."

"Good," Pearce said, not sure whether that was good or not. "Is it loaded?"

"Thirty-two round mag," Joe-Bob said.

Pearce thought for a moment. "Two seconds?" he said. "That all I've got?"

Joe-Bob chewed his bottom lip, then said, "You want to shoot in little bursts. You don't want to hold the trigger down for two whole seconds."

Pearce nodded, put his hand in the bag.

Joe-Bob clamped his fingers round Pearce's wrist and said, "Money first."

Graveyard Shift
Midnight

At the trading estate where Pearce was to meet Banksy, there was a group of units down one side: car repairs, photographers, tool hire, curtain and blind fitters, fridge repairs, that kind of thing. There were other units opposite, a line of small brick buildings. Between them, an area of open ground, apart from a massive warehouse near the entrance to the estate.

The warehouse was half-demolished. Pearce could see what was left of it in the moon-light as he came up to the gated entrance of the estate. A staircase stood on its own, leading nowhere. The warehouse had been gutted, its insides spilling out, the near side of it knocked to the ground. Heavy equipment was dotted around. If you ever fancied hot-wiring a digger, or buggering off with a free cement mixer, here was a chance going a-begging.

Pearce was arriving later than he'd have liked. Would have been nice to have arrived early, scoped the place out.

The gate was open, and a fuck-off padlock lay in the grass. Token security. Couple of seconds' work with a bolt cutter. Pearce noticed that the mesh fencing around the site was loose, too.

Banksy was already here.

Well, Pearce was ready. He'd got the fire-power he was after. In the bag, ready in case he needed it. He didn't want to use it. Just wanted to make the point that he could do some serious damage if he wanted to.

No sign of Banksy.

But Pearce was being watched. He could feel it.

He took a look around, then stepped forward, past the warehouse, onto the road to the right. Strolled past the first of the small brick buildings, his breathing loud in the darkness.

Lights came on. Dazzled him. He screwed his eyes up, shaded them with his hand.

Car head-lights, most likely.

Then Banksy's voice, maybe twenty feet away: "Glad you could make it."

Pearce nodded. Couldn't see Banksy. Couldn't see anything.

Could hear, though. Footsteps approached Pearce from behind. He turned. Able to see again with the lights behind him. Big guy,

gun drawn, silencer on it. No mask this time.
Probably one of the guys who'd whisked Julie
away earlier. "Got to pat you down," he said.

Pearce shrugged. Held his hands out to
the side, still clutching the tool bag.

The guy frisked Pearce carefully. Wasn't
new to the job, you could tell. "Let's see in
the bag," he said.

"You get to see in the bag when Julie
walks," Pearce said.

The guy said, "Fuck that. Let me see in
the bag." He pointed his gun at Pearce, held
it an inch from his head.

Pearce said, "You hear what I said?"

The guy stood for a moment, not sure
what to do. "Banksy," he shouted. "He won't
let me look in the bag."

"Is he clean?" Banksy shouted back.

"Yeah," the guy said.

"Then let him go, Jack," Banksy said.

Jack. Julie had talked about him. Jack Bower. Banksy had a brother as well, Ray. Pearce fully expected he'd be hanging around somewhere, too. Wouldn't want to miss all the fun.

Pearce faced the lights again, shaded his eyes, peered.

Jack Bower pushed him in the back, said, "Move."

Pearce didn't think about it, just slammed his head backwards. Hit something solid with the back of his skull. Heard Jack say, "Ooof."

"Pearce!" Banksy shouted. "What the fuck did you just do?"

Pearce ignored him as he swivelled round and kicked an already stumbling Jack in the side of the head. Jack went down, sprawled on the ground, lay still.

His gun lay inches from his hand. Pearce kicked the gun out of his reach just in case he woke up any time soon.

"Pearce!" Banksy shouted again. "Leave him!"

Pearce stood where he was. Still couldn't see shit.

"Get away from him!" Banksy said.

Pearce strode forward. Kept going till he'd covered half the distance between him and Banksy.

"That's close enough," Banksy said.

Pearce stopped, waited. His eyes hurt.

The lights dipped.

Slowly, Banksy came into view, his arm held out, the gun at the end of it pressed under Julie's chin, forcing her head back as he moved her into position directly opposite Pearce. Banksy's gun was fitted with a silencer, too.

"Now, give me the money," Banksy said.

"Let her go," Pearce told him.

"Pearce," Julie said, her voice shaking. "Please give him the money."

"Shut up," Banksy said.

"Let her go," Pearce said.

"Money first," Banksy said.

"No deal," Pearce said.

Banksy shook his head. "You do have the money, don't you?"

"Let her go," Pearce repeated.

"Do you?" Banksy said. "I fucking hope you do."

"Oh, Christ," Julie said.

"You want to see it?" Pearce said. He didn't wait for an answer, unzipped the bag, pulled out the Uzi, let the bag fall. He pointed the gun at Banksy, finger itching to squeeze the trigger. He heard a noise behind him, a slight thud. Fuck. Pretended he hadn't heard it. Got ready to roll out of the way. For now, he had to make it look as if he was focusing on what was in front of him. Just looking at Banksy and Julie. "Now let her fucking go," he said.

"Such a shame," Banksy said. "I had high hopes we could settle this without blood-shed."

"We can," Pearce said. He heard another noise behind him. A scraping. Like ... wheels crunching gravel. A car. Lights off. Engine off. Free-wheeling towards him. Trying to sneak up on him, catch him out. The road sloped downwards, but it levelled off pretty quickly, so the car would come to a stand-still soon enough.

Well, he knew it was there so that should help.

"Yeah?" Banksy said. "I'm listening."

"Tell whoever's behind me to stop the car," Pearce said.

Banksy asked, "What car?"

"Just tell him to stop the fucking thing," Pearce said.

Banksy shrugged. "OK," he said. He shouted to the driver to put the brakes on.

The sound behind Pearce stopped, but he kept his eyes on Banksy, hard to drag them away from the gun under Julie's chin. "You want twenty grand, right?" Pearce said.

"Yeah," Banksy said.

"Here's my proposal, then," Pearce said.

"Oh, you have a proposal?" Banksy said. "That's fucking posh."

"Yeah," Pearce said. "Lend me the money."

Banksy laughed. "Now that's funny."

"I'm serious," Pearce said. "You can lend me twenty grand. You're a loan shark, right? I give it back to you, plus I pay you all the interest. Everyone wins."

Banksy looked thoughtful. Then he smiled.

Pearce felt something hard press against the back of his neck. Then a click. Fuck, the driver had got out of the car, crept right up behind him and he hadn't noticed.

Fuck, fuck, fuck. He should have been paying attention.

"Nah," Banksy said. "No deal."

"Banksy," Julie said, her head tilted backwards with the pressure of the gun under her chin. "It makes sense."

Banksy shot her.

She swayed. Then fell onto her side.

Banksy said to Pearce, "You got any other proposals?"

Pearce let out a strangled yell, lifted his Uzi. At last, he was sure that Julie wasn't pulling a scam on him. Took a lot to get through his thick skull. But now it was too late.

"Drop it, pal," the man behind Pearce said, pressing the gun hard against the base of his skull.

Pearce recognised the voice from earlier. This joker was the gunman who'd fired a shot into the tarmac at Pearce's feet when they'd bundled Julie into their car.

Pearce thought about pulling the Uzi's trigger. Holding it down for two whole seconds. Firing every one of those thirty-two rounds. Filling Banksy full of holes.

He thought about it. What would happen then? How would it feel to have a bullet enter the back of his head?

He thought about it. But that was all he did. He lowered his arm. Let it dangle. Dropped the gun.

"Good boy," Banksy said. "You want to pick that up, Ray?"

"Can do," Ray said. "Where's Jack?"

Banksy said, "Pearce caught him with a lucky head butt. Jack's lying in the road back there."

"Oh, shit," Ray said. "Is that what that was?"

That bump. That little thud that Pearce had heard.

Could it be?

"What?" Banksy said.

Ray said, "I think I might have run over Jack."

"Jesus fucking Christ," Banksy said.

"I couldn't see shit," Ray said. "No fucking lights. Wasn't expecting Jack to be lying in the fucking road, was I?"

"Go take a look at him," Banksy said. "Did you at least get the kids OK?"

"No problem," Ray said. "They're in the back of the car with the stupid-looking dog."

"What about their granny?" Banksy asked.

"Put up a bit of a fight," Ray said. "Had to tell her I'd chop off another finger."

"Did you?" Pearce said, turning to speak to him.

"Didn't have time," Ray said, bending over Jack's body. "Just gagged her and tied her up."

Nice, Pearce thought.

And all in front of the kids.

But that was nothing to them having just seen their mother being shot.

12:15 am

Banksy walked towards Pearce, bent down, keeping his eyes fixed on Pearce's, picked up the Uzi.

"Very nice weapon," Banksy said. He stepped back. "Shat my pants when you pulled that out, I don't mind telling you. Serious hard-ware. Seen a few Mac 10s around, but not one of these babies. Worth a few grand, too."

He aimed it at Pearce's chest. "Makes up a bit for you not bringing any money with you." He shifted his aim to Pearce's head. "Can you think of a single good reason I shouldn't empty this into you?"

From behind Pearce, Ray said, "Banksy, Jack's not breathing."

"Shit," Banksy said. "Shit." He let his arm drop to his side. "Can you get him in the car?"

"Tight fit with those kids in there," Ray said.

"I meant my car," Banksy said. "In the boot."

"OK," Ray said. "Might need a hand, though."

Banksy said, "Pearce, you've been granted a moment longer. Would you be so kind?"

Pearce wondered what Banksy would do if he said no. Shoot him, then help Ray carry Jack himself. So Pearce walked towards Ray. It was a good call.

He'd only taken a few steps when a sharp crack split the night air. He thought he'd been shot. Then remembered that Banksy had his Uzi, so he'd very likely have heard more than one shot being fired. And Pearce didn't feel any pain anywhere. A second crack. Again, no pain. Sounded like it came from over by the warehouse.

Pearce turned to see Banksy drop to his knees, stare at his chest.

"Ray," Banksy said. "Ray! Some fucker's shot – " He fell forward onto his face and was still.

"What the fuck?" Ray said, running towards him.

Pearce grabbed Ray's arm as he passed, twisted his wrist hard enough for Ray to drop his weapon and scream.

Pearce picked up the gun.

"Ow, man," Ray said. "That fucking hurt." He was holding his sore hand in the palm of his good hand.

Pearce pointed the gun at him.

"Oh, shit," Ray said. "I'm sorry, pal. Honest. Don't kill me, pal. Don't."

"Your brother's dead," Pearce said. "If I leave you alive, you'll come after me."

"No," Ray said. "It's cool. I wouldn't. Me and Banksy, we weren't all that close." He was shaking. "Didn't like him all that much. He was a bastard. Honest. He was my brother but I thought he was a cunt."

Pearce took a deep breath. "Hold your hand out," he said.

"You what?" Ray said.

"Hold your hand out," Pearce said. "There's something I have to do."

Ray cottoned on. "Ah, fuck, no, I need my fingers. No, you can't – " He stuck his hands behind his back.

"Fair enough," Pearce said. He shot Ray in the foot. Then he shot him in the other foot. Then he shot him between the eyes. Ray fell on top of his brother. One dead cunt on top of another.

12:20 am

Pearce looked towards the warehouse. Waiting to see who the shooter was, the one who'd taken out Banksy. He had an idea who it might be.

But nothing moved.

Maybe the shooter had already gone.

Left Pearce to clean up.

Before he did that, he had to check on the kids.

12:21 am

When Pearce opened the back door of the car, Hilda jumped up at him, licked his hand. Pearce tickled him under the chin and said, "Everyone OK?"

Kirk said, "I don't like Ray. I think he's gay, Pearce."

"Yeah," Pearce said. "Don't worry about him." Then he noticed what Ray had done and thought that maybe Ray hadn't been such a cunt after all.

Ray had hung a black cloth from the roof of the car. It divided the front from the back, and also meant that the kids, who were strapped into their car seats, couldn't see out. They hadn't seen any of the shootings. Hadn't seen their mother killed. That was something.

Maybe Ray had done it to protect them. Or maybe he'd done it 'cos he didn't want to be bothered seeing them while he was driving.

Pearce would never know.

Devon said, "You got fireworks?" She yawned. "I hearded them."

"Only one or two," Pearce said. "They're all done now."

"Oh," Devon said. "I'm tired. I want to go home."

"I have to tidy up here first," Pearce said. "Give me a moment."

12:25 am

He'd taken his gloves off and put them on Jack. He'd got Jack's coat off and was now struggling to remove Jack's jumper when he saw the figure standing by the warehouse. Didn't so much see it, as saw it move. Coming towards him.

As it got closer he saw the gun. A rifle. Slung over the shoulder.

He ignored her. He had to hurry.

He got the jumper off with a final tug. Jack's body slumped forward, the neck lolling at a strange angle. Pearce couldn't work out whether the car had broken Jack's neck or crushed his wind-pipe. No matter. Either way, he was dead. Pearce took his own sweater off. Put Jack's on himself. Nice fit. Both of them were built on the hefty side. Slipped on Jack's coat. Only thing left was to get his own sweater on Jack.

"Pearce," she said. "What are you doing?"

"You should get out of here," he said. They were still twenty feet apart.

"I will," she said. "But I thought you might need a hand."

"Haven't you done enough for one night?" he said. He sounded angry. Actually, he was angry. She'd taken a massive risk. But he was also grateful. "I'm sorry," he said. "I should say thanks."

"It's OK," she said. There was only five feet between them now.

"Why?" he asked her, pulling his sweater over Jack's head.

She said, "I owed you."

"Ailsa," he said. "What happened before, that was years ago. Anyway, I did it 'cos I wanted to." He forced Jack's left arm through the hole in the sleeve.

"Because I couldn't do it myself," she said.

She'd tried, though. Bought herself a gun, just couldn't get hold of any ammo for it. She'd changed since then. Changed big time.

"Different story now," Pearce said. "When did you learn to shoot?"

"Joe-Bob's been teaching me for a while now," she said. "Says I have a gift."

"Ailsa," Pearce said. "You ever shot anyone before?"

She looked at Pearce struggling with Jack's other arm. "Yeah," she said. "Once."

Pearce was surprised. She'd changed all right. "Who?" he said.

"I could tell you," she said. "But then I'd have to kill you." She didn't smile. "You need help dressing that guy?"

"No," Pearce said. "Don't get your DNA on him." He forced Jack's arm through the sleeve. A gloved hand popped out and Pearce pulled it through.

Done.

Jack was wearing Pearce's jumper. Jack was wearing Pearce's gloves. Maybe the forensic team would believe that Jack was the one who'd fired the gun. Maybe not, but it was the best Pearce could do.

"How about Banksy?" he asked Ailsa.

"What about him?" she said.

"You shot him," Pearce said. "How do you feel?"

"Fine," she said. "I was just planning to give you some cover. But when I saw what he did to that woman, I got pissed off."

Pearce didn't know what to say to her. He thought he knew her, but all he knew was what she once was. This was someone else. He'd liked her before. Now he liked her all over again. Damn it.

"Those kids I saw earlier," she said. She looked over towards Julie's body. "Is that their mother?"

"Yeah," Pearce said. "Their father's dead too. But they don't know it. Not yet. Their granny's still alive, though. At least they have someone. Listen, you should go."

"What are you going to do?" she said.

"Wait for the police," he said. "Work on my story while I'm waiting."

"But you shot one of them," she said. "You have to go."

"I didn't shoot anyone," he said.

"I saw you," she said.

"You were never here," he said.

"It won't work," she said. "Swapping your clothes won't fool the police."

"It might," he said. "Pile of scum like these three, they won't look too hard for anything other than easy answers."

"Is there blood on those clothes you've just put on?" she asked.

"Shit, I don't know," Pearce said. "Can't see in this light. But it doesn't matter. Jack was run over. Probably got tyre marks on his throat. And the kids know Ray was driving the car. So unless the police decide I head-butted Jack to death and he died of a bleeding nose, I'm safe enough."

Ailsa asked, "But if Ray was the guy driving the car, how could Jack have shot him?"

Good question. Pearce thought about it. "I'll say Jack lived long enough to shoot Ray," he said. "The point is, Jack's wearing gloves that'll have traces of gun-shot on them. It's my word against his and he's not in a state to speak for himself."

"It's risky", she said. "Why don't you just leave?"

"The kids," he told her. "They know my name. They know I was here."

"You're fucked if you stay," she said.

"I'm fucked if I don't," he said. "Just go, Ailsa. I'll be fine."

She said, "I wish I could do something."

"You can," he said. "Take the Uzi with you, give it back to Joe-Bob. I might be a little

tied up for a while. Now go. Get the fuck out
of here."

She turned.

"Hey, Ailsa," he said. "Thanks."

12:30 am

Pearce got inside the car. As he pulled down Ray's black cloth, Hilda leaped into the front.

"Pearce?" Kirk asked.

"Yeah?" he said.

Kirk said, "Did you find my mummy?"

"Mummy!" Devon said.

Pearce looked straight ahead. Couldn't make much out. He'd turned out the lights of Banksy's car, put Jack's coat over Julie.

"Yeah," he said. "I found her."

"Where is she?"

"Somewhere nice," Pearce said. "But far away. She has to stay there a while."

"I don't want her to," Kirk said.

"But you get to stay with Granny," Pearce said. "Won't that be fun?"

"Ray tied her up," Kirk said.

"Funny game," Devon said.

"Yeah, it was just a game, Devon," Kirk said. "Granny said."

"I know," Devon said. "Where's Daddy?"

Pearce lowered the window, heard sirens approaching. "Look," he said.

"Police," Kirk said.

"Police!" Devon said.

"Yeah," Pearce said. "Police. Devon, you think you can wave your magic wand and make them go away?"

Want *more?*

Dead Brigade

by

James Lovegrove

A new kind of soldier ...

This is the British Army of the future. Soldiers brought back from the dead to fight as robots.

The zombie army can learn.

They can kill.

The only thing they can't do is die.

Even if they want to ...

Want *more?*

Revenge

---

by

Eric Brown

Dan's got everything – and everything to lose.

Dan Radford has it all. He's a pro footballer with a big house, fast cars, cash – and a drink problem.

But the star striker is dragged into a nightmare of violence, kidnap and blackmail.

Dan has an enemy – and he's out for revenge.

Want *more?*

Heroes

by

Anne Perry

Murder on the battlefield.

It's the First World War. Men are dying every day.

Hundreds of them, sometimes thousands.

But one death is different. One death is murder. How important is one murder among all the other dead?

How far will Joseph go to find the killer?